What Matters Most

Emma Dodd

templar books
an imprint of Candlewick Press

What matters most of all to you?
What matters most to me?
Let's take a look around us,
and maybe we will see.

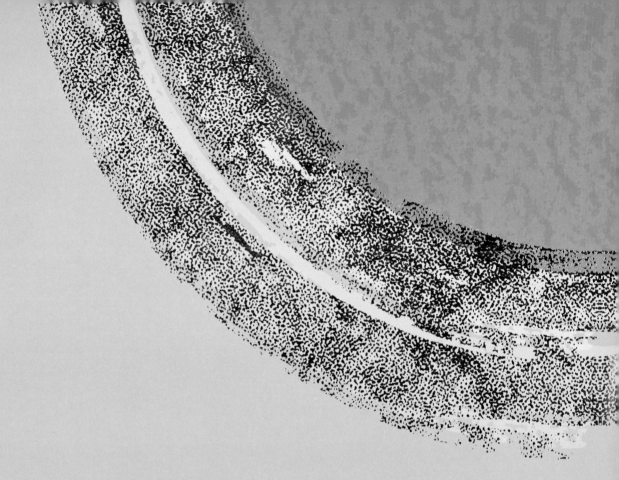

Is it being very big,

or being super small?

Is it having lots of stuff,
or not that much at all?

Is it talking all the time,

or making time to hear?

Is it being really brave,

or sometimes feeling fear?

Is it being in a crowd,
or spending time alone?

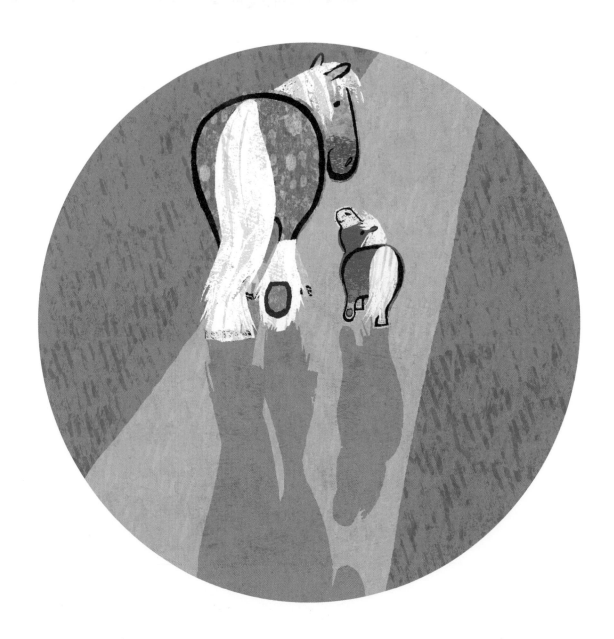

Is it always going out,

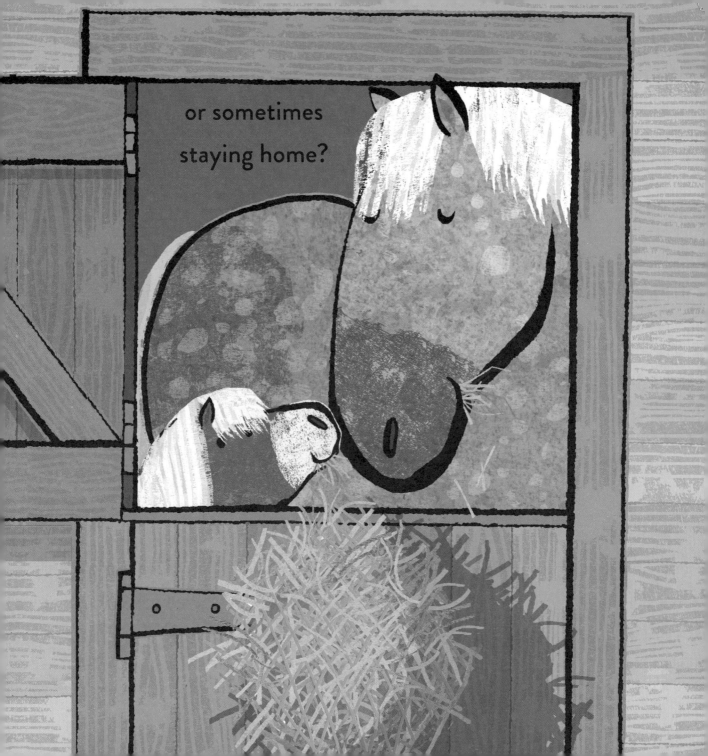

or sometimes
staying home?

Is it going very fast,

or just taking it slow?

Is it knowing
everything,
or the things we
don't yet know?

Whether you are scared or brave,

or if you're big or small . . .

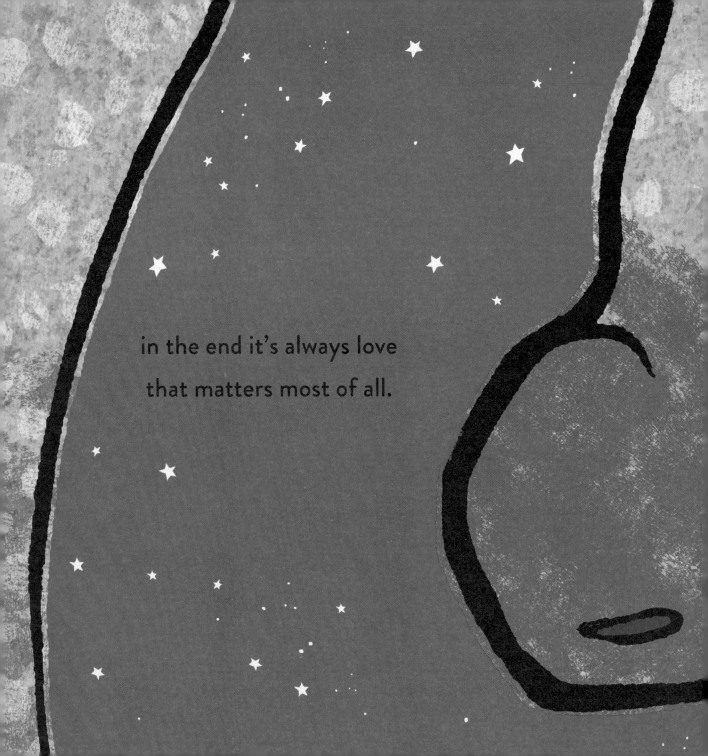

in the end it's always love
that matters most of all.

First U.S. edition 2020

Library of Congress Catalog Card Number pending
ISBN 978-1-5362-1017-0

20 21 22 23 24 LEO 10 9 8 7 6 5 4 3

Printed in Heshan, Guangdong, China

This book was typeset in Eureka Sans.
The illustrations were created digitally.

TEMPLAR BOOKS
an imprint of
Candlewick Press
99 Dover Street
Somerville, Massachusetts 02144
www.candlewick.com